Lucy was very excited when she woke up.

That IS exciting, Lucille. But how do you plan on finding a new friend?

Lucy's search got off to a great start when a nice critter invited her to play.

Ooh ooh, YES! I'd love to join you!

Ribbit!

It didn't take long for Lucy to find another friendly-looking animal.

That friendship didn't work out either.

She asked lots of questions.

And she tried to fit in with everyone she met.

But Lucy was starting to feel ridiculous.

She came close to making friends a few times.

Thanks for inviting me to lunch!

But something always went wrong.

Lucy couldn't believe how hard it was to make a new friend. She was ready to be friends with ANYONE.

Well, almost anyone.

SQUEAK!

SQUEAK.

That's when things got ugly.

Lucy tried to calm
herself down.

It looked as if Lucy would never find a new friend.

And that's the story of how these two friends found each other.

The End

For my oldest friend, Mike

—P.B.

Little, Brown and Company • Hachette Book Group • 237 Park Avenue, New York, NY 10017 • Visit our website at www.lb-kids.com • Little, Brown and Company is a division of Hachette Book Group, Inc. • The Little, Brown name and logo are trademarks of Hachette Book Group, Inc. • The publisher is not responsible for websites (or their content) that are not owned by the publisher.

First Edition: September 2011 • 10 9 8 7 6 5 4 3 2 1 • SC • Printed in China

ISBN 978-0-316-07030-0

The illustrations for this book were rendered in pencil on paper, with cut construction paper and wood and a wee bit of digital tweaking. The narration text was set in Clarendon, and the word balloons were handlettered by the author.